KATIE WOO
and PEDRO
Mysteries

The Peanut Butter and Jelly Mystery

by Fran Manushkin

illustrated by Tammie Lyon

PICTURE WINDOW BOOKS
a capstone imprint

Published by Picture Window Books, an imprint of Capstone
1710 Roe Crest Drive, North Mankato, Minnesota 56003
capstonepub.com

Text copyright © 2023 by Fran Manushkin
Illustrations copyright © 2023 by Capstone

Library of Congress Cataloging-in-Publication Data
Names: Manushkin, Fran, author. | Lyon, Tammie, illustrator.
Title: The peanut butter and jelly mystery / by Fran Manushkin; illustrated
by Tammie Lyon.
Description: North Mankato, Minnesota : Picture Window Books, [2023] |
Series: Katie Woo and Pedro mysteries | Audience: Ages 5–7. | Audience:
Grades K–1. | Summary: Katie's peanut butter and jelly sandwich is
missing, so she must figure out which of her classmates ate it—and what she
should do about lunch.
Identifiers: LCCN 2021048201 (print) | LCCN 2021048202 (ebook) |
ISBN 9781666335736 (hardcover) | ISBN 9781666335682 (paperback) |
ISBN 9781666335699 (pdf)
Subjects: LCSH: Woo, Katie (Fictitious character)—Juvenile fiction. | Chinese
Americans—Juvenile fiction. | Hispanic Americans—Juvenile fiction. |
Theft—Juvenile fiction. | Sandwiches—Juvenile fiction. | CYAC: Stealing—
Fiction. | Sandwiches—Fiction. | Chinese Americans—Fiction. | Hispanic
Americans—Fiction. | Mystery and detective stories. | LCGFT: Detective
and mystery fiction.
Classification: LCC PZ7.M3195 Pad 2023 (print) | LCC PZ7.M3195 (ebook) |
DDC 813.54 [E]—dc23
LC record available at https://lccn.loc.gov/2021048201
LC ebook record available at https://lccn.loc.gov/2021048202

Design Elements by Shutterstock: Darcraft, Magnia
Designed by Dina Her

Printed and bound in the USA.   PO4882

Table of Contents

Chapter 1

Looking Forward to Lunch

It was ten o'clock. Pedro told Katie, "I'm hungry. I can't wait for lunch!"

He looked into his bag. "Yuck! It's tuna fish. Maybe I *can* wait."

Katie gave her lunch
bag a pat. "I have a peanut
butter and jelly sandwich.
Dad put lots of grape jelly
on it. *YUM!*"

During recess, Katie and
Pedro and JoJo ran around
and had a blast.

As they walked back to class, Katie said, "All that running made me hungry. I can't wait to eat my sandwich!"

But Katie got a surprise:

Her lunch bag was gone!

"Oh no!" she said.

"Somebody took it."

Chapter 2

Where's Katie's Sandwich?

Katie looked at Roddy. He

was always taking her pencils.

"Your fingers are purple,"

said Katie. "Did you take my

sandwich?"

"Roddy didn't take it," said Pedro. "His hands are purple from his leaky marker."

"Oh," said Katie. "I see!"

Katie looked at Pedro.

"You told me you don't like

tuna fish for lunch. Did *you*

take my sandwich?"

"I'm your friend," said

Pedro. "I would never do that."

"You're right," said Katie.

"I'm sorry!"

Pedro pointed to a brown

paper bag on JoJo's desk.

He asked, "Is that Katie's

lunch?"

No! JoJo was going to use
the bag to make a mask for
a party.

Barry was holding
something brown! Was it
Katie's lunch?

No!

It was a sock puppet
Barry was making for art.

Chapter 3

Mystery Solved!

Katie went to get her paints
for art. When she came back,
there was a paper bag on her
desk.

"Your lunch is back!"

yelled Pedro.

Katie gave the bag a pat.

The bag wiggled!

"Yikes!" yelled Katie.

"Sandwiches do not wiggle."

Katie peeked into the bag.

She saw something green.

Was it a pickle? No!

Katie opened the bag.

Something jumped out.

It was a frog! The frog

croaked and hopped out the

window.

Katie laughed.

Roddy laughed louder.

Katie looked at Roddy.

He had a brown paper bag
on his desk.

"Roddy has purple lips,"
said Pedro. "They are the
same color as grape jelly."

"Roddy took your lunch!"

said Pedro.

"I did!" said Roddy.

"I forgot to pack mine. So I

traded you a frog I had for

show-and-tell."

"Frogs are fun," said

Katie. "But not for lunch."

Katie giggled. "No way

for lunch!"

"You can share my lunch," said Pedro. "You will be doing me a favor."

He gave Katie half of his tuna fish sandwich.

It was a very happy lunch!

About the Author

Fran Manushkin is the author of Katie Woo, the highly acclaimed fan-favorite early-reader series, as well as the popular Pedro series. Her other books include *Happy in Our Skin*, *Plenty of Hugs!*, *Baby, Come Out!*, and the best-selling board books *Big Girl Panties* and *Big Boy Underpants*. There is a real Katie Woo: Fran's great-niece, but she doesn't get into as much trouble as the Katie in the books. Fran lives in New York City, three blocks from Central Park, where she can often be found bird-watching and daydreaming. She writes at her dining room table, without the help of her naughty cats, Goldy and Chaim.

About the Illustrator

Tammie Lyon, the illustrator of the Katie Woo and Pedro series, says that these characters are two of her favorites. Tammie has illustrated work for Disney, Scholastic, Simon and Schuster, Penguin, HarperCollins, and Amazon Publishing, to name a few. She is also an author/illustrator of her own stories. Her first picture book, *Olive and Snowflake*, was released to starred reviews from *Kirkus* and *School Library Journal*. Tammie lives in Cincinnati, Ohio, with her husband, Lee, and two dogs, Amos and Artie. She spends her days working in her home studio in the woods, surrounded by wildlife and, of course, two mostly-always-sleeping dogs.

Glossary

clue (KLOO)—something that helps someone find something or solve a mystery

croak (KROHK)—the low, echoey sound that some frogs make

mystery (MISS-tur-ee)—a puzzle or crime that needs to be solved

trade (TRADE)—to exchange one item for another

wiggle (WIG-uhl)—to make small movements from side to side

All About Mysteries

A mystery is a story where the main characters must figure out a puzzle or solve a crime. Let's think about *The Peanut Butter and Jelly Mystery*.

Plot

In a mystery, the plot focuses on solving a problem. What is the problem in this story?

Clues

To solve a mystery, readers should look for clues. What are some of the clues in this mystery?

Red Herrings

Red herrings are bad clues. They do not help solve the mystery. Sometimes they even make the mystery harder to solve. What clues in this story were red herrings?

Thinking About the Story

1. What are some things Katie did to find her missing lunch? Make a list of five ways someone can find a missing item.

2. Imagine you are Katie. What would you do if your lunch was missing? How might you react? Write a paragraph.

3. Do you think Roddy's show-and-tell item was a good trade for Katie's lunch? Explain why or why not.

4. If you could make the most epic sandwich ever, what ingredients would you add? Draw a picture of this sandwich and write down the steps to make it. Share with a friend.

Mystery Sandwich Test

Using clues and his sense of sight, Pedro solves the mystery of the peanut butter and jelly sandwich. With this fun sandwich test, you can test your friend's and family's other senses to see if they can guess the ingredients! Make sure your friend or family member isn't allergic to any of the ingredients you use.

What you need:

- 12 crackers or 6 mini buns

- blindfold

- a friend or family member

- your choice of ingredients, such as tuna, jelly, peanut butter, mayo, cheese, pepperoni, ham, olives, apples, cucumbers, carrots, tomato, pickles, hummus, cream cheese, etc.

What you do:

1. Get two crackers or one mini bun.

2. Place any two or three ingredients you choose inside the two crackers (or one bun) to form a sandwich. For example, you can make a peanut butter, apple, and marshmallow sandwich or a sour cream and onion sandwich.

3. Repeat for five more sandwiches.

4. Then, place the blindfold over your partner's eyes. Make sure they don't peek.

5. Give them one sandwich at a time and let them investigate what the mystery ingredients are.

Solve more mysteries with Katie and Pedro!

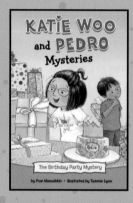

KATIE WOO and PEDRO Mysteries
The Birthday Party Mystery
by Fran Manushkin • illustrated by Tammie Lyon

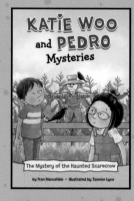

KATIE WOO and PEDRO Mysteries
The Mystery of the Haunted Scarecrow
by Fran Manushkin • illustrated by Tammie Lyon

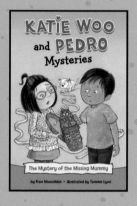

KATIE WOO and PEDRO Mysteries
The Mystery of the Missing Mummy
by Fran Manushkin • illustrated by Tammie Lyon

KATIE WOO and PEDRO Mysteries
The Mystery of the Snow Puppy
by Fran Manushkin • illustrated by Tammie Lyon

KATIE WOO and PEDRO Mysteries
The Mystery of the Stinky, Spooky Night
by Fran Manushkin • illustrated by Tammie Lyon

KATIE WOO and PEDRO Mysteries
The Peanut Butter and Jelly Mystery
by Fran Manushkin • illustrated by Tammie Lyon

KATIE WOO and PEDRO Mysteries
The Rainbow Mystery
by Fran Manushkin • illustrated by Tammie Lyon

KATIE WOO and PEDRO Mysteries
The Super-Duper Supermoon Mystery
by Fran Manushkin • illustrated by Tammie Lyon